AND THE MOON FOLLOWS

CYN BERMUDEZ

An imprint of Enslow Publishing

WEST 44 BOOKS™

Please visit our website, www.west44books.com.
For a free color catalog of all our high-quality books,
call toll free 1-800-542-2595 or fax 1-877-542-2596.

Cataloging-in-Publication Data

Names: Bermudez, Cyn.
Title: And the moon follows / Cyn Bermudez.
Description: New York : West 44, 2021.
Identifiers: ISBN 9781538385296 (pbk.) | ISBN 9781538385302
  (library bound) | ISBN 9781538385319 (ebook)
Subjects: LCSH: Sexual abuse--Fiction. | Family--Fiction. |
  Friendship--Fiction.
Classification: LCC PZ7.1.B476 An 2021 | DDC [F]--dc23

First Edition

Published in 2021 by
Enslow Publishing LLC
101 West 23rd Street, Suite #240
New York, NY 10011

Editor: Caitie McAneney
Designer: Seth Hughes

Photo Credits: Cover (sky) Utthapon wiratepsupon/
Shutterstock.com; cover (moons) Elena11/Shutterstock.com.

Printed in the United States of America

CPSIA compliance information: Batch #CW20W44: For further information contact
Enslow Publishing LLC, New York, New York at 1-800-542-2595.

For Mom

CHAPTER ONE

Mornings at my house are always buzzing with activity, especially on the first day of school. The earthy scent of coffee wakes me and I check the time. Ten minutes before my alarm. I turn it off and pull the covers over my head. I want to fall back to sleep, but I hear feet shuffling busily, socks on wood. Next, I hear the thump of shoes. I remove the covers from my face and open my eyes. Light filters into my room, creating lines of shadow as the light seeps through the blinds.

My younger brother and sister are awake. They always seem to be in unison. They have been since birth, being twins and all. They move about the house together fussing over everything–shoes, hair, clothes. Their outfits usually match. I hear them at the table, pouring cereal, spoons clanking. Right now, they're excited about the first day of school. I wish I could say the same.

Finally, I stumble out of bed. My morning ritual is the same, school or not. I head straight for the kitchen and pour myself a glass of orange juice. The cold, tangy juice helps me start my day. The twins are already at the table.

Mom bought the twins matching khaki pants and white polo shirts. My sister, Sophie, has a pretty pink headband over her short hair. Mike's hair is short on the sides. The top is gelled into a wave. Their hair is the only difference between the two. They're fraternal twins, but their face structure is almost identical.

As for me, I think the first day of school is overrated. And it's not because I don't like school. I actually *like* learning. I'm just not interested in the "who's got more" dance. My wavy hair hangs over my shoulder. My bangs, which I trimmed last night, are slightly skewed. I have my outfit laid out on my bed—my favorite vintage *Goonies* T-shirt with a hole in the lower right corner, and of course, my favorite jeans, the ones I've had since the seventh grade. I've sewn them several times. Multicolored threads are stitched awkwardly down the thigh area, where my pants always rip. I aim for comfort over pizzazz.

"Morning, brats," I say.

The twins are on their phones playing a game. Sophie and Mike look up at me.

"Good morning," they say.

Mike returns to his game but Sophie stares at me for a bit. I wonder what she's thinking.

"What?" I ask. I assume she's checking out my clothes. My little sister is... *fashion sensitive*. She takes after our mom in that way. Worries about hair, clothes, and shoes–too much if you ask me. Hope, my best friend, is similar, so I'm used to it. I clarify, "This is *not* what I'm wearing to school."

I'm wearing pajamas! Still, I feel I have to state the obvious.

"Can you blame me for wondering?" Sophie says.

She's so snarky for a nine-year-old.

A horn honks outside. The twins begin to rush. One last spoonful. Their spoons ding against the bowls. Their uneaten cereal begins to turn to mush. Leaving early in the morning is normal for them. The twins play sports with the same groups of kids. Last year, the parents took turns giving rides to school. The same for this new school year. The twins gulp the rest of their juice. Their plastic cups are on the table at the same time. Their chairs scrape across the kitchen floor. I actually feel a gust of wind as they run for the door.

My phone chimes. Hope texted me her outfit. Brand new dark-colored jeans. An off-white peasant shirt. Short-sleeved with puffy shoulders.

Hope sends me another text: "Please tell me you're not wearing those god-awful jeans!"

I text her back: "@@." Rolling my eyes emoji.

Just then my stepdad, Frank, walks into the kitchen.

"Always on that phone, Luna," he says.

He heads straight for the coffee. His hair is slicked back with the same gel Mike uses.

"No, I'm not," I say.

He doesn't look at me. Instead, he fixes himself a cup of coffee. The coffee is set on a timer. Mom prepares it before she leaves to work at night. If my mom doesn't premake the coffee, it doesn't get made. At least not by Frank. I'd have to do it. And if not me, Sophie would have to make coffee if he wanted it bad enough.

"You set the example for your sister and brother," he says.

It bugs me that he thinks he knows what's best. He entered our lives permanently a couple of years ago. What does he know? Nothing.

"Why do they even have phones?" I ask. I seriously get blamed for everything around here.

"Don't sass me, girl," Frank says. His Okie accent is strong despite his efforts to sound "Hollywood," as he puts it.

He gulps down the rest of his coffee. When he finishes, he sets his cup down on the counter. I place my glass in the sink and head back to my room.

Frank calls after me, "Where you goin'?"

I ignore him.

Back in my room, I put on some music. I like classic rock. Hope calls me old. On my phone, I stream one of my favorite bands. The volume is low enough I can hear Frank as he approaches my room. He's on one, for sure. He gets in these moods where all he does is complain. I feel like he picks on me more than the twins. Maybe because they're younger.

I grab the doorknob, intending to shut the door. He blocks the door from closing with his foot.

"What do you want, Frank?" I say.

I know I shouldn't talk back. Frank told my mom it's 'cause I'm "half beaner." He said, "It's in her DNA to be trouble. Just like her father." One time he said I needed to be more Asian instead of Mexican. I wanted to scream, "Asia is a freaking continent!" More often he says I need to be more "China." I'm not even Chinese. For the record, my mother is Filipino, my dad Mexican.

I push on the door, trying to force it shut.

"I'm really tired of that mouth," he says.

He pushes his way into my room.

Startled, I apologize. "Sorry," I say.

My face must look like how I feel. A sense of worry washes over me. His face softens.

"Relax," he says, with condescension. But it also feels like a threat.

He's standing too close. I turn my back to

him and walk toward the outfit on my bed. "I need to get ready for school."

He doesn't leave at first. He walks up behind me. I feel his hot breath on my neck. My muscles stiffen. His hands are on my shoulders. I'm motionless. I move away from him and stand by my dresser pretending to look for something.

The hum of a car interrupts the awkwardness of the moment. Mom is pulling into the driveway. The car door opens and slams shut. My bedroom door squeaks and closes. Frank is gone. I hear keys rattling at the entrance. The front door opens and shuts with a soft bang.

Mom is home.

CHAPTER TWO

P.E. is my first class, which I hate. My hair frizzes from sweating. The fresh soapy scent of my morning shower becomes wasted and replaced by an outdoorsy one. I even tried not to run too fast, hoping I could stop my sweat glands from kicking into overdrive. Luckily Hope brought her flat iron to school. She's always prepared like that. Makeup, flat iron, a change of clothes—I swear she's a walking fashion show. I was able to fix myself to an almost-pre-P.E. state.

"Thank God for all that junk you bring," I say. I tug at her backpack. Luckily her next class is nearby.

"Preparation is the key to success," she says, smiling as she walks away.

Hope is always ready with some sort of "key to success." I think she takes her name way too seriously. Besides, if her name makes her hopeful, what does mine make me? My name is Luna, like the moon.

These are things I think about when my class is a yawn like history, which is right after P.E. and my most boring class. My teacher talks so slowly, I struggle to pay attention. Time moves painfully slow. Is it possible to sleep with your eyes open?

Next I have English with Mrs. Kuhn. I don't think it'll be too bad. I like reading, and having your best friend in at least one class feels like it should be law. Hope and I must talk too much, though. Mrs. Kuhn, a short woman with a high-pitched voice, seems annoyed with us. I'm usually the quieter one, but Hope is silly. I can't help it if she makes me laugh!

"So... did you talk to Damien?" she asks in a whisper. There is a playfulness in her voice.

My cheeks are flushed red. I've been crushing on Damien since freshman year. If he ever looks in my direction, I might turn redder than a cherry.

"No," I say and signal a shush.

Hope rolls her eyes. "I mean, what's the deal? Just tell him you have an arrow for his bow."

Hope is guffawing a little too loud. It's my turn to roll my eyes.

I mouth a "ha ha."

Damien is kind of bowlegged and Hope likes to tease me because of it. But I think it adds to his cuteness.

"Too bad he isn't in English with us this year. I'd definitely have to get him to notice you. Hypothetically speaking, it could involve cartwheels. Mrs. Kuhn might literally have a cow," Hope says.

I actually think Hope is serious. She just pretends to kid around.

The walk home from school is the best part of the whole day. First, because school is over. Second, because Hope and I talk about our day. Hope lives a few blocks down from me. We arrive at my house first. Dread washes over me. I'm not good at hiding things from Hope. She looks at Frank's car in the driveway and then back at me. She gives me a tight hug.

"Only five hundred and sixty-seven days," she says. "Then you'll be eighteen. Only five hundred and seventy-three days if you wait for me. Which you will, of course. Then we can kick our fake parental units and fly this coop."

"That's assault," I say.

"More like self-defense," she says.

She's kidding, of course. Our only plan is to move far away from this dinky little town. Far away from my stepdad. Far away from her mother's boyfriends. We want to live in a big city, like New York.

"Your stepdad and Valerie's chump of the month should..." Hope begins her usual rant.

This is where Hope's language gets a bit *colorful*. She calls her mom Valerie instead of Mom. They're even poorer than we are. Her mom drinks a lot and gets colorful with her language too. You wouldn't know Hope's life from Hope alone. I only know because we've been best friends for as long as I can remember.

I interrupt her. "Hope."

"Uh? Oh yeah, sorry," she says. "I just get so

mad."

"I know," I say.

"You should just talk with your mom," Hope says. "She's not like *Valerie*."

I shake my head. I can't talk to my mom either. She's always gone. Working or whatever. And when she's home, she has her family. *Them*. Frank and her other kids. The twins aren't Frank's, but they might as well be. They're more accepted than I am. Besides, she doesn't listen to me anyway.

"Only five hundred and sixty-seven days," Hope says again.

"Five hundred and seventy-three days," I say, correcting her.

"Of course," she says.

We say our goodbyes and Hope continues to walk down the sidewalk to her apartment. I turn toward the front door of my house. I take in a deep breath. I walk as slowly as I can.

Frank is in a mood. His angry, creepy mood. No telling what he'll do when he's like that. I have to be careful with how I speak, walk, breathe. If my freaking hair sways the wrong way. Seriously.

I reach the door and turn the knob as quietly as I can. I set my first foot in like a cat. Once I'm in, I shut the door quickly. I need to head straight to my room. I try to not think about my actions because that's when I mess up more. Become louder. Clumsier.

I put my headphones in my ears as if they're a barrier to the world outside. I think about school. By far my favorite class today was physical science with Mr. Christianson. He started the school year with astronomy. Today, we learned about stars and how they were formed. The difference between a constellation and a star system. A constellation is a group of stars that forms a picture in the sky. A star system contains one or more stars that orbit each other. He showed us the Centauri star system. It's the closest to the Earth next to our sun. Alpha Centauri is the largest star in that system. But Proxima is technically closer to the Earth.

"If Proxima Centauri is the second closest star to us, what's the first?" Mr. Christianson asked with a lisp. He paced the room, his deep red hair in a comb-over. He smiled with cleverness as if anticipating his "gotcha" moment. "I'll give you a hint: Proxima is the closest to the

Earth in the Centauri constellation."

"The sun, duh," a girl said. I've seen her before. She's dark-skinned and chubby, and I can already tell she's one of the "smart kids."

"You are correct!" he said.

Then, the last bell of the day rang. I hear the same bell now in my head. The loud piercing sound. I pull the headphones off my ears.

I'm at my door. Inside my room. I try to shut it. Frank is there at my door again. He blocks the door from closing with his foot.

"What are you doing, Frank?" I say too loud, too angry.

I'm alarmed and afraid. My heart is pounding like crazy. The harder I push the door, the harder he pushes back. He overpowers me and the door flings open. He pushes the door with a lot of force. The knob crashes into the wall and breaks through the plaster.

"You got a real problem today, don't you?" he says. Frank hates it when he feels like he's being disrespected. Which is all the time. Today he seems to be more irritated, angrier.

"Get out of my room," I yell back.

He puts his hands on my upper arms and

pushes me up against the dresser and then to the bed. This is worse than anything that's ever happened before, and I see it coming before it does.

I try to fight, to struggle. He's too strong, too heavy. I close my eyes. I smell alcohol and aftershave. I taste heavy cologne in my nose and mouth. I feel the slime of his hair gel across my cheek.

He's on top of me, and suddenly I'm millions of miles away. Proxima Centauri. It's the nearest star, a red dwarf, 4.244 million light-years away from Earth.

The front door opens and I hear the twins. Mom follows in after them. She's putting grocery bags on the counter. Mom is home. *Mom is home.* She calls out for Frank. He leaves my room in a hurry, buttoning his pants.

Without a word, I walk into the bathroom, my school clothes in my hand. I shower for a long time. When I'm done, I go back into my room and sit on the floor, shaking. Mom is in the kitchen. I don't come out for dinner. I wonder if she'd know. If she'd see the difference in me. She doesn't. She doesn't even notice.

CHAPTER THREE

The next day, I hear everyone in the kitchen preparing for school and work. I wait until they're gone before I leave my room. By late morning, Hope is blowing up my phone. She writes the same message but in different ways. This time she says, "Where are you? You better not be ignoring me, *loca.*"

I don't respond. I don't know what to say to her or to anyone.

The house feels different. All the lights are off but the darkness isn't serene. The stillness isn't comfort.

I'm in the kitchen staring at a cutting knife in the drawer. I don't know for how long. A distant honking horn pulls me back to the present. I slam the drawer shut. I open the fridge door and devour a leftover cake my mom brought home from work. Then leftover pizza the twins had. A bologna sandwich and some chips. Two glasses of milk. I eat until I feel full, but there's still a hollow space.

I shower again, for a really long time. I cry. More like sob. The shower is the only place I feel safe to let my tears out. When I finish, I sit on my bed in a towel for a while. I see the light of my phone, hear its ding. My room is not my own. Not anymore. It feels like a cage. And suddenly I know that if I stay, I'll be trapped. I will be prey, over and over again.

I wish my dad were here. He would believe me. But he's been dead for years. I can't tell my mom. She loves Frank. She'll believe what he says. I know I can't stay. It would kill me.

I panic. I jump quickly and dress. I run back to the kitchen for a trash bag.

Back in my room, I quickly gather a couple of outfits, socks, and underwear, and toss them into the bag. I grab my physical science book and the small teddy bear Hope gave me for my tenth birthday. That's it. I'm moving so fast, I don't stop to think. I put on my shoes, pick up my small trash bag of stuff, and I leave.

☽

I don't know where I'm going. Somewhere between my house and school, I come out of the haze. There's an apartment complex across the street from my high school. I'm hiding out in the parking lot waiting for the bell to ring. A heaviness washes over me. A knot tightens in my stomach. What did I do? Why do I screw everything up?

I hide my bag in the large trash bin, placing it in one corner, so I can get it later. When the bell rings, I rush to join everyone else spilling over into the halls. Hope is nowhere in sight. I beeline it to my physical science class—my last class of the day. I'm a few seconds late.

I'm the last one to walk into the class. Mr. Christianson is at the board. We're learning about when stars die. If a star has enough material, it explodes. Like three times the material of our sun. It's called a supernova. And all the elements are made either inside the star or when it explodes. Every element that makes up the planets, air, water, animals, even people, come from stars. It's amazing really. For a moment, I forget everything else. I wander among the star stuff traveling through space.

Class is over. I take my time stretching the last minute of the hour.

"Everything all right, Luna?" Mr. Christianson says.

I want to tell him everything, but I don't. How can I? Then he'd know how messed up my life is. How messed up I am. I'm already invisible. I don't need to be a freak too.

"Yes. I, uh, just liked the class today. Stars and all that," I say.

Mr. Christianson smiles excitedly. "Wonderful."

"So we really don't have homework?" I ask. I'd take the syllabus out and show where it says that. But I forgot my binder and backpack at home.

"Nope. None. Don't believe in it. Your home-work is your first science paper and presenta-tion. Have you thought about what you want to do? I know school just started but I have some slots filling up already. It's not far off."

"Um, not really. But probably this," I say. I point to the notes on the board. "This astronomy thing."

"Excellent. I'll put you down for 'the astronomy thing,'" he says and chuckles.

I'm about to walk out, but Mr. Christianson stops me. "Are you sure everything's okay?" he asks again.

My chest gets tight. My stomach is heavy. I swallow back the tears. "Yeah. Yes."

CHAPTER FOUR

"Where the heck have you been?" Hope asks as we leave school.

"Heck?"

She shrugs. "I'm on a language diet."

When I chuckle, I choke a little on my saliva. I cough for a few seconds. "Language diet?"

"Whatever. You know what I mean. I don't know if you notice, but I cuss like a... like a... cowboy in a saloon."

I can't help but laugh, and for a moment I forget what happened. My mouth is open. Slapping my knee and everything. Hope gently shoves my arm and rolls her eyes. "Yesterday, when I got home, I crept in quietly so Valerie wouldn't bother me. She was talking with the chump of the month, using such vile language. I swear it was like hearing her for the first time. I thought, 'Do I sound like that?' and was like 'Oh he—,'" she says. Hope puts her hand on her hip. She fake coughs. "I mean heck nah."

"I don't mean to laugh, Hope," I say. "Positive change is positive. Just, you know, good luck with that."

"Thanks for believing in me," she says, rolling her eyes.

I put an arm around her. "I *do* believe in you."

"So what's the deal with you? Where were you today?"

Reality rushes back to me. I avoided Hope because I knew... I knew I'd need to tell her. I couldn't hold it in anymore. The tears came out quiet but uncontrollably.

"Whoa, what's going on? You're scaring me," Hope says.

"Not here," I say. I don't wait. The last thing I want is for others to hear. I start walking to the apartments across the street, right to the trash bin where I hid my bag of stuff. I hear Hope calling after me, but I don't stop.

"Luna!" Hope says. "Wait."

I grab my bag out of the trash bin as soon as I get there. I turn and face Hope. I wait for her to finish walking the distance between us.

"What is *that*?" she asks, pointing to the bag. "Did you kill someone?"

I'd be offended if there wasn't a look of part-terror and part-sarcasm furrowing her perfect brows. She always makes me laugh. Sad, angry, scared—and she is still the funniest person I know.

"Dork, no." I look at the ground. To her feet. Then to mine. How do I explain to her what happened? I don't want to think about it anymore. Just forget it. Sweep it away. I struggle for the words.

"Something happened," she says.

I feel her eyes examining me. Observing my face, my body. I swear it's like she can read my mind sometimes. She knows. I don't even have to say anything. She wraps her arms around me and gives me a tight hug.

"I'm leaving. Not goin' home," I say.

"But where?" she asks.

"I don't know. I haven't thought that far ahead," I say.

"You're coming home with me," she says.

I can't help it. I start to cry again. It's like all the things I don't say just escape through my eyeballs.

"I know what you're thinking, Luna. Listen, Valerie's boyfriends are pervs, especially this current one. Sorry. But you don't have anywhere else to go, so you're coming home with me. We'll just stay away from them." Honestly, Hope's home life isn't much better than mine. Might even be worse.

"Okay," I say. "Sorry."

"Don't be," she says.

)

Hope's room is like the contents of her bag—organized with everything she might need. Tons of blankets and stuffed animals. A long mirror from the 99-cent store hanging on her closet door. Her dresser has matching knobs, unlike mine. She was happy when she found them at Gundies for a quarter. That's what we call the segunda, the secondhand store. On top is her makeup. Mostly stolen, but there's some she saved up for and some that I bought her for birthdays.

"Your mom might call Valerie, so I'm not going to tell her you're here," Hope says.

"I figured," I say.

I can tell she has more to say but is hesitating for some reason.

"Just spit it out," I say.

"You gotta sleep in the closet."

CHAPTER FIVE

Hope's closet already seems small and jam-packed with her clothes and shoes. It's worse having to lay down inside of it. I even try to distract myself with my science book. I'm on the chapter about Newton's Laws. The Law of Gravity and the Laws of Motion. I just started on the first law of motion. An object like a ball will stay still until something hits it. Same in reverse. It'll keep moving until something stops it.

I get distracted by some kind of commotion in the living room. I can't really hear what they're saying. Only raised voices. Something about "my stuff."

Hope's mom doesn't have very much. She has a little two-bedroom shack near the projects.

Sometimes she's a waitress. Sometimes she's a heath care aid.

Hope doesn't have money for all the crap she has. She stole a lot of it. I've been with her. Though I can afford a little more than she can, I stole with her. We have a whole technique down.

When we first started lifting our clothes, we wore big, baggy dresses and slipped on clothes underneath. We'd layer them, looking puffed up and obvious. How we didn't get caught, I will never know. I mean we looked like we had on three or four layers of clothes. But then Hope got smart. She worked briefly for a department store and took their magnetic strip remover. Her wardrobe boomed after that. She'd offer me two empty shoeboxes for hiding the goods. She had the other two. She carried them in shopping bags so it looked liked we'd already checked out. I didn't wear most of the clothing she got me. I had my own style. But she grabbed stuff I liked too. Plus the books I wanted. I miss my books.

And shoes. OMG. The amount of shoes she has should be illegal. Well, it actually *is* illegal.

Hope left to use the bathroom and grab me

some food. She's gone for a long time.

Finally, there's a light knock on the door. The doorknob turns slowly as if to keep quiet. Hope's dirty laundry is nearby so I rush to pile it on top of me. My face is covered by the hanging clothes. I take a deep breath in and hold it.

I wonder if maybe it's Hope trying to frighten me. But my gut tells me to wait. There is silence. Then the closet door opens a nudge. I hear the hangers scoot. The metal hook scrapes against the wood. My heart is pounding in my chest. I can't hold my breath any longer. I want to let it bellow out of me like a storm. But if I do, I'll be caught. Hope's mom may be drunk, but she knows how to dial a phone. She'll call my mother in a heartbeat. Instead, I let the air from my lungs slowly. A little bit at a time. God, it hurts.

The person at the closet lets out a light sigh. I can smell perfume now. It must be Hope's mom. What the heck is she looking for? She exhales again with a forceful blow. Now a tinge of alcohol makes its way to my nostrils. The woman drinks all day and all night. I don't think I've ever seen her sober. And her moods intensify and change depending on how much she's had. One minute she's forcing Hope and me to sing her favorite Peter, Paul and Mary album. I know all the words to "Puff the Magic Dragon." And "I'm Leaving on a Jet Plane." God, that one is burned into my brain. She often yells, "Again, again!" Like a small child. The next minute she's yelling and smashing bottles, accusing Hope and me of getting into her stash. I swear we don't touch her stuff.

She's getting frustrated. She scoots a large section of clothing to the side. My face is exposed! Oh crap. My body is shaking. This is it. I close my eyes as if that will make me invisible.

"Oh, *come on,*" Valerie says.

I close my eyes tighter, bracing myself. She'll yell. I know it. But then I hear the door shut. Hope's mom has left the room.

Relief rushes through me. I sit there for a moment to relax. All of a sudden, the smell of Hope's gym socks overpowers the leftover perfume. I push the clothes off of me and jump up. It dawns on me that maybe she saw me. Valerie might have called my mom already. Oh my God. My mom might be on her way. Or worse, she might be here already. Pulling up into the driveway. Or in the living room accepting tea from a drunk woman.

I gotta get out of here. I check the window. Hope has one of those locks on it. I try to twist it off, but it's stuck. I try again and my fingers slip. I'm half tempted to throw her alarm clock through the window. Then the door opens.

CHAPTER SIX

I exist for a moment in the in-between. In that split second where I am both dead and alive. A cat in a box whose fate is about to be revealed. It's the longest freaking second, but also the fastest.

I brace myself for whoever is about to open the door.

The door opens. Hope walks in. She lifts her index finger to her mouth and shushes me.

When the door is shut, I whisper to her, "Where were you? Your mom was in here."

"Shh," she says again as if I need reminding. "I know. She insisted I took her stupid sweater."

"I thought we were caught," I say.

"Nah, she's completely toasted." Hope lifts

her hand, pretending to hold a wine glass. She pretends to drink from it.

"I know. I smelled the alcohol from under your stinky clothes," I say.

"Stinky? Pff. You mean the delicate scent of roses," she says.

Now we're both laughing. In her hands, she's carrying a napkin stuffed with food.

"This is the best I could do," she says.

She shoves the food into my hands. In the napkin are two pieces of bread and a cold drumstick of fried chicken. I don't even care. I'm so hungry. I eat without pause.

We stay up late. Talking about boys. Damien. And the different guys she likes. I think I fall asleep first.

🌙

I'm up early in the morning. I'm reading my science book in the closet. Newton's second law of motion was tricky at first. But I imagine the movement of a ball, like a basketball. The ball will move faster the more I push on it. That's the force I put on the ball, but that changes if Hope pushes on the ball in the opposite direction. Whoever is stronger wins. But the movement of the ball depends on both of us. If the basketball becomes a bowling ball, I would have to push harder because there is more material smashed together. It doesn't matter that they're the same size.

Hope startles me. Her face is an inch away from mine, her nose almost touching my cheek.

"Whatcha doing?" she asks playfully.

"Science," I say. I lift up my book.

"Uh, nope," she says, and grabs my book from my hands.

"Hey!" I protest.

She puts a hand on her hip and tilts her head with attitude. "You're such a nerd."

"Nerds rule the world," I say.

Hope starts laughing as if I said something too stupid. "No, rich white men do."

I roll my eyes and grab my book from her. I know all too well how white men rule, but I say, "Don't burst my bubble."

"You know you don't have to keep sitting in the closet when no one's here."

As soon as she says it, our heads snap to

attention. We give each other that look. The one where your ideas and your best friend's ideas are the exact same. The idea: Hope and I are ditching school. I say, "I can't go to school. My mom's been blowing up my phone. I'm sure she's already contacted them. You don't have to stay with me... unless you want to."

I wait for her to respond. She's busy putting on mascara. Her top lip curls over her teeth as she spreads the black goop on her eyelashes. I wonder if my mom has called her mom. Of course she has, but I suspect Hope won't mention it. Not right now. She doesn't want me to worry unless there's something to worry about.

"Duh," she says finally. She takes out an old DVD of *The Little Mermaid*. We both start laughing.

"Really?" I ask.

"It's either this or I get to do a makeover on you," she says.

Hope is serious. She's ready to strap me into the bed and force-feed me Disney cartoons while coating my eyelids with generous amounts of purple eye shadow. I'm not going to fight her on it. Not really. I pretend to protest a bit but cave eventually. Honestly, I'm grateful she's here with me.

I don't want to be alone.

◡

Hope swears I look great, but I feel uncomfortable. I wanted her to stop a few minutes ago when she started contouring. She's all Bob Ross on me now. My face is a canvas. She's applying happy little clouds onto my eyelids. Seeing her happy makes me happy too. So because of that, it's worth it. When she finishes, she observes me like I'm her masterpiece.

"Please let me take a picture?" she asks again.

"As long as you don't post it," I say.

"Fine. Whatever. I promise," she says.

She snaps a picture with her cell phone. A few minutes later, I take my phone and double-check all her social media accounts. Just to make sure.

A notification comes through my phone. A friend request from Damien. Hope and I take a peek at his photos. He's so cute.

Later, I'm in the closet reading my science

book. Taking notes for my presentation. I know I don't have to. Especially since I don't know when I'll be back to school. But I like it. And it takes my mind away from my life. I'm reading about momentum. My eyes get heavy. It is the end to an almost-perfect day.

But then Hope reminds me to wash my face. Reminds me how important it is to take care of my skin. She follows to make sure I clean my face right.

Hope and I are in the bathroom when Valerie and Rudy, the chump of the month, arrive. Luckily the door is locked when Rudy starts banging on it.

"Gotta pee," he screams. His words are slurred.

"I'm in here," Hope screams back.

She signals for me to hop into the bathtub. I shake my head furiously. Hope lifts her hands, palms in a "what can I do?" gesture. My eyes widen. Are you freaking kidding me? But I do what she says. She's right. I'm in the bathtub when she walks out and Rudy walks in. The shower curtain is drawn. And once again, I'm stuck.

CHAPTER SEVEN

Hope finally tells me her mom is riding her about me. I knew my mom must have spoken to hers, but now the school is involved too. They're watching Hope more closely, so now she can't ditch anymore.

Being alone in someone else's house always gives me a weird feeling. Like peeking into someone else's life when they're not looking. Hope's home is a small shack of an apartment. They own a brown plaid sofa, one leg propped up with a folded piece of cardboard. There's a single green lamp and one of those boxy TVs. The mantel is littered with photos. Most of them are ancient. Black and white or a yellowish-orange tinted color. Sepia I think it's called. At least according to my Instagram photo filter. The photos are probably of relatives like grandparents and aunts. But there are also photos of Hope when she was a baby and a toddler. And photos of her mom, Valerie, as a young woman. There's one of Valerie as a teen in a cheerleader outfit.

I thumb through Valerie's old yearbook. Seems like she was popular in high school. A lot of people signed her yearbook. There are a lot of pictures of her too, mostly in her cheerleader uniform. She was even prom queen. I wonder if the prom king is Hope's dad. They have the same chin and high cheekbones. The same eye shape.

Hope is at school. She couldn't ditch another day. I don't know where Valerie and her boyfriend are. I take advantage of the time outside of the closet. I'm reading my science book in the living room, learning about the relationship between heat and temperature. Basically, the hotter something is, the faster the motion of its molecules. A good example is air. Hot air moves fast and expands. Temperature is a measure of that heat. I wish I had a highlighter so I could highlight certain sentences. All I have is a pen.

My stomach grumbles. The refrigerator is

newly filled. Lots of ground beef and drumsticks in the freezer. Weenies and bologna in the fridge. Cans of tomato sauce and *fideo* on the counter. No quick fixes, which sucks. The quickest thing I can think of is a flour tortilla with butter.

I heat one up on low heat. The refrigerator door is open, butter in my hand, when I'm startled. Keys are jingling at the door. Someone's home. I toss the butter back into the fridge. Slam the fridge door shut. I rush to the room.

I'm about to hide in the closet, but decide under Hope's bed is better. It's Valerie. She's on the phone talking with someone about a bill. Burning tortilla hits my nostrils, and I remember I forgot to turn off the stove. Dang it.

There's silence. No doubt Valerie saw the burning tortilla. Hope's bedroom door flies open. Trying not to breathe, I inhale and exhale slowly.

"Hope?" Valerie says. "You best not be playing hooky."

There's more silence. I hear her feet walking away from the room. Doors opening and shutting. Her feet coming back this way.

"Who's here? Hope is in school. Come out or

I'm gonna call the law."

She waits what feels like an eternity. She leaves in a huff. My heart pounds in my chest. I gotta do something. I slip out from under the bed. The faster I try to move, the heavier my body feels. Like in a horror film. The window I'm running toward seems miles away. I finally open the window. There's a screen. I have no time to think. No time to find an alternate route. I'm like the air trapped in a bottle. Heat rising. My molecules speeding away from each other. From me. I push the screen out like a jar bursting open. I jump to the ground. I don't look back. My only focus is to get as far away as I can.

I finally slow down when I get to the train tracks a few blocks from Hope's. My phone vibrates in my back pocket. Thank God I have my phone! It's Hope.

"Oh my God! Are you okay?" she asks.

"Uh, no. I left my book in the closet!" I say. I'm still out of breath.

"That's what you're worried about?"

"How did you know what happened?"

"Hello! My mom is blowing up my phone!"

"I'm sorry, Hope."

"Don't be," she says. "But I'm not sure what's going to happen when I get home."

CHAPTER EIGHT

I hide out for a while by the train tracks. An hour later, my phone finally buzzes again.

Hope whispers, "Valerie is on one. I think the whole mess might have even sobered her up a bit. She actually said she's grounding me. Like she *never* grounds me. She saw you running from the house. Called your mom, the school, *and* the police!"

"I ran fast! What about my stuff?"

"I hid it. But I have to lay low until she's plastered again. I'm sorry. Stay by your phone! I have to be careful. She forgot about my phone, but if she sees me on it, she might get motherly again and ask to see it. I delete everything you send right away, just in case." We hang up.

It's hard to know what to do with myself. Where can I go? I have nowhere. It'll be dark in a few hours. I need to figure something out. First things first, I disable location services on my phone. Hopefully, no one can track me now.

A car alarm beeps on. My stomach grumbles. Louder this time. I'm starving. There's a grocery store on Union. The Green Frog Market. I walk fast, avoiding main roads. I cut through parking lots and alleyways.

When I get there, it's nearly empty. Only a few customers are inside—a single cashier, the meat guy, and Mr. Reyes stocking. I need to make sure to stay away from that aisle. He's ancient and knows everyone in town. His hair is whiter than snow. His skin is more wrinkled than a raisin.

I stay away from the meat guy too. I don't know his name, but I've been in here plenty of times with my mom. I don't want to risk it.

The Green Frog Market is big. Not as big as the chain superstore. I'm extra careful. I don't really like stealing, especially from here. I feel guilty enough about the clothes Hope steals for me. But Hope wouldn't have clothes if she didn't steal them. I don't think her mom has bought her anything since she was eight.

I feel less guilty about stealing food. So much is thrown out. If I grab the ready-to-toss food, why does it matter? Why not just give the food to those who need it?

I've only taken what I've needed when times are thin, and always from the ready-to-throw section.

The ready-to-throw section is between the bread aisle and canned veggies. It's a white rack pushed up near the entrance to the bathroom, right next to the fridge where the ready-to-throw cold items are. Slim pickings today. Some powdered donuts. Bread. But luckily there's bologna and almost-expired milk in the fridge.

I don't have a bag, which sucks. I can't go through the front door holding stolen food. There's the emergency exit. But there's an alarm attached to that one.

There are brown double doors nearby. They lead to the back. Suddenly I notice the rest of the customers around me. The mom with her chubby kids putting stuff in the cart when she's not looking. The old man shuffling his feet way too slow for the young woman behind him. She's clearly on her break. They don't notice me, not yet. The main problem is the meat guy.

My stomach growls again. I grab what's there: the milk, bread, bologna, and powdered donuts. My heart starts beating fast. My thoughts fade. It's just me. The lights of the grocery store. The brown doors. Electricity runs down my spine. I bolt for the doors.

The heaviness is back in my knees and feet the moment I start to run. In my side vision, I see heads turning, fingers pointing right at me, mouths opened in confusion. I run like I have cement shoes. But it's as if nothing else exists. Only the vacuum of space. The Earth rushes toward me. Through atmosphere. Clouds. Over the ocean. The green of open land. The park bench.

I'm so parched, my throat feels sticky. I cough and cough until I catch my breath. The sun has set. Only the last colors of dusk paint the sky, a beautiful purple-orange hue. I make two sandwiches. I wolf them down and gulp down the milk.

My eyes feel heavy when I see something. An outline of a figure. There's someone in the distance. I recognize his legs. The way he walks.

Bowlegged. I fall off the park bench and hit the ground hard. It's Damien. He's walking his dog. My leg is hurt. It's hard to get up quickly, so I crawl and hide behind a nearby tree. I would hate for him to see me like this. I know I'm not as fashionable as Hope, but even I know how I must look. Bad enough I'm full. My leg hurts. And now my stomach is gurgling.

It's almost completely dark when I leave the tree. I walk into the nearby neighborhood. I have no plan. No idea what I'm doing next. I just start checking car doors. Hoping. I don't want to sleep outside. The first car I try is a blue Ford. It's locked. About a dozen or so cars later, I find one. A rusted Dodge. It's unlocked. I wonder if my heart literally stops for a moment. I hope there's no alarm. There isn't. I climb inside.

When I finally exhale, darkness dominates the night. It's cold. An autumn haze settles onto the ground. I'm shivering. The silence is creepy.

The blue light from my phone shines onto the ground. I try to find anything to cover the light and myself. I find a sweater. I use it first to cover the light of my phone. My phone dings. Hope finally texts.

CHAPTER NINE

After school, I meet Hope at the park. I'm worried about getting caught if I go back to our neighborhood. I'm far enough here, safer. I see her sitting. She's waiting for me on the same bench I was at the day before. I limp my way to her. She notices.

"Long story," I say as I approach her. I point to where Damien was. "Damien. He was walking his dog. I was hungry and scarfing food, and well... now look at me."

Hope chortles. "I can guess what happened."

I roll my eyes. Hope hands me a plastic grocery bag. Inside are my clothes and my science book.

"My book!" I say, relieved.

"I also brought you a brush. Toothpaste is in

the baggie. A bar of soap and shampoo in the small plastic bottle. And a traveler hairbrush. I figured you're probably ripe."

I laugh. "Yeah, just a bit. Any news?"

She nods. "I heard your mom posted online. She's asking anyone if they've seen you."

"Oh no. Now I really gotta lay low."

"Or you could just go home. Talk to your mom."

"Don't do that. You know I can't." My eyes tear up.

"No," she says. "Not really. I don't know why you can't. You haven't told me anything. I know it has to do with Frank. He's a creep, so I can guess, but that's not the same as knowing."

I'm silent for a while, unsure of how to respond. I don't even know if I can say it out loud. "I know. I just... it's difficult."

"All right," she says. She gives me a tight hug. "You don't have to say anything. I just want you to be okay."

"Hope, he forced–" I try to say more, to explain more, but I can't. The words are lodged at the base of my throat, threatening to steal the breath from me if I speak the truth. The intensity of the moment turns awkward.

Hope changes the subject. "There's an abandoned house not far from here. I checked it out already. No electricity or gas, but there's still running water for some reason. I snuck over some blankets and a pillow."

"An abandoned house?"

She nods. "It's better than a car. Do you want me to go with you? I can show you where it's at."

I want her to stay with me, but how can I ask her that? Her home life isn't great, but I can't just ask her to leave. To live on the streets. Or in a car. Or in an abandoned house.

"No," I say. "Just tell me where it's at. I'll find it. I'll be okay."

Hope gives me a guilty look. "Are you sure?"

"Yes. Really. Go home before sober Valerie shows up."

She walks with me for a few blocks. Then we part.

☽

The house is almost unnoticeable. Small and guarded by a chain-link fence. The street is the last in a tract. The house is at the end. Open fields line the back of the homes, making it look rural. The windows are boarded up. The paint is a bit chalky. But other than that, it's pretty sturdy. The roof is intact, and the walls too.

I enter through the back so no one sees me. There's dust everywhere. The living room is creepy. The carpet is stained and musty. The kitchen is bare. Cabinets open. There's no sink or stove or fridge.

There are three rooms. In one of the smaller rooms is the stuff Hope left. Two blankets, a pillow, some canned food with an opener. She left more bread and water. She even left me candles for light. If there was a way to turn the electricity on, she would. And Hope wouldn't be Hope if she didn't leave something to clean with. There's a cheap broom, cleaning solution in a spray bottle, and a rag.

One room looks like she already started cleaning it. Of course, she picks the best room in the house for me. Not too dark. The boards don't cover the windows all the way, so enough light gets in. The room is in the back and faces the open fields.

I'm in for a long day. I take out my notepad and start writing my presentation. My day alternates between reading about electricity and writing. At some point, it gets too dark to read or write. And then I hear a noise. I text Hope.

"Like what?" she texts back.

"Scratching... and creaking. What if someone's outside?" I text back.

"Stop worrying so much. It's a pretty quiet area. Don't freak out," Hope texts.

My battery is on 11%. Preserving my battery is the smarter choice. Hope's right. I just need to go to sleep. I blow out the candle. Say a little prayer. *Please don't let there be a crazy killer outside my window.*

The scratching is rhythmic and steady, like a tree branch against the roof. It starts to soothe me after a while, the way rain does.

CHAPTER TEN

I wake in the late morning. The scratching sound is gone. I hear other sounds, like cars passing by and a dog barking in the distance. I spend most of the day cleaning. Not just my room but also the rest of the house.

Thank God there's a bathroom, and even though there's no logical reason for it to have running water, I'm so happy it does. Comes in handy when I have to pee in the middle of the night. Though toilet paper would be nice too. I have to remember to ask Hope to bring me some. I sweep everywhere I can and wipe every wall.

At some point, I run out of cleaning solution, but I still wipe down the walls and counters. I do this for hours. It's like I'm running as fast as I can. From everything. From my life. If I stop... even for just a moment...

If I stop, I don't think I can stand it. The weight of everything. Of Frank. Of what happened. It will crush me. I don't think I'll survive. I don't want to know anymore. I want to forget. If I can just keep going...

My arm starts to cramp. There's a light knock and the sound of the door opening.

"Hey," Hope says. "How was your first night? I see you survived the scratching."

I look away. My eyes are watery. I pretend to laugh. "The scratching really was scary."

"You okay?" she asks. Of course she notices. Hope notices everything.

"I'm fine."

"Luna," she says. Her voice tells me she knows I'm lying.

"Don't."

There's silence for a few long seconds. I feel bad. I know she cares.

"Oh. Look what I brought you."

I'm grateful she changes the subject. Hope digs into her backpack. She holds up a paper print of flowers in a vase. They're pink and yellow with green stems.

"Wonderful," I say. I pretend not to care. She knows I'm kidding, but she plays along.

"It's art! Your place needs a little color."

My place. I like the way that sounds. If only this house really were mine.

"A lot of people asked me if you're okay. Even Damien."

"He what? What did he say? Oh, my God. Tell me everything." Suddenly, we're ourselves again.

"Okay. It was so random. I was eating lunch. I didn't even notice him at first. All of a sudden, he was standing next to my table. He said, 'I hope Luna is okay.' Then I said, 'Me too.' Because I don't want to risk telling anyone I know where you're at. Even Damien."

"Of course! So he knows who I am... *Wow*."

"I know, right? He knows your name. And he cared enough to ask. I couldn't wait to tell you."

I try to show more enthusiasm, but I can't.

"Now I know you're not okay," Hope says.

"Just because I'm not googly-eyed over some stupid boy?"

"Luna."

"I'm... sorry. Can we just talk about something else?"

"Okay," she says. A mixture of worry and defeat is in her voice.

"What if this were our place?" I change the subject. I try to sound happy. "What would we decorate first?"

The next few days are calm. Almost happy. Hope comes by after school. She brings me food from the cafeteria. She gets a free lunch, so she shares half with me. She also brings more cleaning products and another print of flowers in a vase. This time they're blue flowers. She tapes it to the wall next to the other one. The concern over my mother's post seems to have died down. I'm just another runaway teen.

I don't mind living like this. There's no Frank. No one to give me crap or hurt me. It's even peaceful. I spend my time working on my presentation or just chilling in the backyard or reading my science book. I've even gotten used to the food—cold leftovers, canned stuff, stale bread with warm bologna.

And Hope remembered to bring me toilet paper. Seriously, you don't realize how important TP is until you don't have any.

CHAPTER ELEVEN

The rustle of the wind wakes me out of deep sleep, where it's just me and darkness and remnants of dreams. The same tree branch is scratching against the roof. It's louder now. The wind whips it furiously. I'm not fully awake until a car door slams. Bright lights sting my eyes open. Suddenly I'm aware of every sound. A CB radio crackles. It's muffled, but it's close enough. My stomach hurts. Worry washes over me.

In the living room, I inch my way to one of the boarded windows. There's a small slit between the boards. At first, I see nothing. Just the front lawn. The house across the street. Then I see him. He's off to the side. His car is parked in the driveway. There's a police officer outside. He's writing something on a pad.

I wonder if someone told, if Hope said something. Maybe she slipped up or maybe she did it on purpose. She has been worried about me, wanting me to talk to my mom, anyone. No, she wouldn't do that. Maybe one of the neighbors saw me?

I can't think about it right now. There's no time. The cop will be inside any minute. I'm sure of it. He'll probably search the whole house. It's not like I can just hide.

I rush back to my room and quickly pack my stuff. I make sure to pack my science book. I wish I could take the blankets and pillow, but there's not enough room in my bag. And they're too bulky to carry. I shove one blanket into my backpack, the lighter one. I move the other blanket and pillow into the closet and close the closet door.

There's no other way out. It's either the front door or the back. I peek outside the room. I don't see a flashlight. Or hear footsteps. I run to the back. Then I take off running through the fields.

I'm in that space again. Running. Nothing else exists. Just the wind and the ground. My body is just a weight that keeps me in this space.

Newton's third law of motion states that

for every action, there is an equal and opposite reaction. Gravity pulls me down. The earth pushes back. It's like how a bird soars through the sky. Their wings push down on the air. The air pushes back. Equal and opposite reaction. I'm caught in the middle, by the laws of nature! By things I cannot control. What is my life if it's not my own?

I'd take flight if I had wings.

I stop when I'm across the field. The house is far enough away. But I'm not quite in the clear.

Then I remember: my presentation was under my covers, my handwritten paper partially covered. The stupid pillow was on top of it. *Maybe I'm wrong?* I frantically look inside my backpack. I pull everything out one by one.

Please be here. Please.

I dump the final contents of my bag onto the ground. It's all the loose junk that usually rattles around in the bottom unnoticed. Pennies and nickels. A button and a paperclip. *Now I find the paperclip. Of course.* I look through my stuff again just to be sure.

My paper is not here. But I knew that already. I only hoped that maybe I was mistaken. I take a long and deep breath.

There are two choices in front of me. Forget the paper. I think most people would do that. Right? Hope wouldn't go back for the paper. The fact I'd risk everything just to get that darn paper makes me the biggest weirdo. Like, who does that?

But it's important to me. More important than a grade. It's like my whole world is riding on that presentation. Not that I ever thought I'd turn it in.

I really have no choice then. I need to go back to get it.

Oh man. My heart is thumping in my chest. I make my way back to the house, fast and in full stealth mode. If I could wear camouflage, I would, but walking low to the ground will have to do. When I make it to the back door, I'm practically on the ground. I lift my head in short, quick bursts. I don't see the cop anywhere. I think he's gone, but there's no way to know for sure from here. I can't see the driveway. His car could still be parked there.

But it's time.

CHAPTER TWELVE

There's no one inside. At least not that I can see. I listen for movement. The silence is unnerving. The hairs on my arms stand on end. After a few seconds, I head toward my room. I take my time, still listening for any sort of movement. A stupid cat outside makes me jump with a *meow* and pitter-patter of its paws. I check every room, carefully. My neck muscles tighten. My shoulders ache.

In my room, everything is intact. Mostly. The flower prints are still on the wall. Cleaning products are still propped up in one corner. But the closet door is *open*. Panic rises up my body. The cop must have seen the blanket and pillow. They don't appear dirty or old. He's a cop. He'd probably notice their clean scent–Hope's favorite detergent. I don't have time to worry about that though.

I search for my presentation frantically. I push the blanket and pillow side to side. I can't find it. Now the panic is in my chest. If it's not here, then he took it. My name is on it. Oh man. *Okay, just calm down.*

I pull the blanket completely out of the closet and give it a good shake. I hold it between my fingertips on one edge and my paper falls out. The pages scatter on the floor.

Yes!

I gather each sheet carefully. I pat them on the ground to even out the edges. I flip through each page to make sure it's all there. Place it in my bag gently. I'm no longer paying attention to my surroundings.

I zip up my backpack when I hear my name. Surprised, I fall backward. It's the cop. My knees go week. He's super close, just a few feet away. I'm stunned. My mouth is dry. I'm unsure of what to do next.

The cop looks just as shocked as I am to find me. We stare at each other, waiting for the other to make their move. I debate what to do in my mind. He's standing about ten feet from the door, just a few feet from me. It's either over right now, or I try to push past him and run.

I feel as if I haven't stopped running since the moment I left my house. The exhaustion becomes all too real, bearing down on me like gravity, that mysterious, seemingly unchanging force. But I find the strength. I have to try, because anything is better than having to go back home with Frank. I quickly calculate the distance from where I'm standing to the door. I'm counting on the cop's great height and weight slowing him down. So...

I *run*.

The panic rises from my feet to my neck to the top of my head. For a second, I think I'm caught. I feel his fingers tug at the shoulder of my shirt. Maybe it's the adrenaline. I read about that last year in bio. Our body makes it when we need to use a lot of strength. It pumps through our blood when we're afraid. Or excited. The more intense the feeling, the more adrenaline is made. No matter the cause, my feet move. I imagine this is what it's like to run on the moon, where gravity is almost a sixth of the Earth's. My legs become long arcs as I speed across the field.

The cop follows me. He's like that cartoon coyote, and I'm the roadrunner. But unlike the cartoon, there's no permanent escape. He's got the advantage. Like most men, it seems, he has the power.

I hear the siren of his car. The whoop-whoop of determination. I stop at the crosswalk. Force of habit. The cop and I lock eyes. Another standoff.

I keep going. I jump over a four-foot brick wall. The wall is long. Thick bushes line the other side, where I land. The wall and bushes enclose a parking lot and a large apartment complex.

I hide behind the thickest bush I can find and wait. I try not to move too much. With my luck, the cop will have super-vision or something. He'll see the leaves and twigs of the bush sway if I move them. I'm afraid to even breathe. It feels like forever. I've been squatting here so long my knees hurt. I think my legs have fallen asleep.

He's turned into the parking lot. The sound

of tires over pavement is unmistakable. He's getting closer because the sound is getting louder. And then the sound hits its peak. I can only see the bottom side of the car. The passenger side. The bottom half of the wheels. The first set. Then the second. The sound of the car fades as it moves away. Even still, I wait, just to be sure. The bush scrapes my skin as I exit from behind it. To be extra cautious, I cut through the apartment complex.

CHAPTER THIRTEEN

I wish I could fall asleep for a hundred years. Dream that I'm happy. The drama of the morning hours has left me exhausted. My bones ache. My muscles too. I want to take a shower—a real, hot shower.

I don't have a destination. I'm just too afraid to stop moving. When I finally rest, I'm at a park near the apartment building across from the high school. I stay safely out of sight, hiding behind the park bathroom, though it's not needed. School is out. I'm not here for anyone in particular anyway. Not even Hope. I'm not watching anyone either. I'm too far away to see detail. I see only the faint outlines of my peers, like people in an oil painting. They're moving about, living their lives. Separate from me. I feel so far away.

The smell of smoke brings me out of my head and back to the moment. I don't turn to look. I only move my head so I can see with my side vision. There's a man standing near me. I get that weird knot in my stomach. I move over, trying not to make it obvious. The scent of the smoke gets stronger. Did he move closer? My palms start to sweat. I scoot over a few more inches.

The smoke is heavy in the air. I cough. He's right behind me.

"What the heck are you doing?" I yell, but I don't mean to.

He offers me a cigarette. He holds out the pack to me. I shake my head.

"Stay away from me," I say.

He grabs my arm from behind and pulls me into the bathroom. "What's your name?"

His hot breath on my neck grosses me out. I try to yank free, but he's strong.

He grabs my other arm. "I just wanna know your name. I've seen you lurking around town. No place to go? I can help you with that."

His breath smells horrible, like rotten food. I use all the strength I can muster to push him back. "No thanks, creep."

I start thinking about Frank's hair gel and the memory of its smell overpowers the smoke. The creep pushes his lips onto my face. The roughness of his five o'clock shadow is on my cheek.

Suddenly, I'm back in my room that day with Frank. I scream and I scream. My fingers dig into the man's face. I pull his hair. Bite his finger. He's yelling now too. He lets go of me and calls me crazy. He takes off like a hurt dog.

Maybe I am crazy. I pick up a rock and throw it at him, and the rock hits his head. I pick another, throw it and hit him again. And another. And another. Until the rocks no longer reach him. Until he's gone.

I collapse to the ground. I sob quietly, my chest feeling crushed with some great weight. I cry till my eyes are puffy. Until I can't cry anymore. I don't know how much time has passed. I know the school is empty now. The sky is turning orange.

"Are you all right, honey?" An elderly woman is looking down at me, a dog leash in her hands. A little furry dog barks at me.

I wipe my nose with the back of my hand. "Yes."

Satisfied with my answer, she leaves.

I leave too.

🌙

The open field by the abandoned house is hilly. The grass is green and uncut. It's a perfect place to hide. No one can see me if I lay on my stomach.

I see the abandoned house but know I need to stay far enough away. I'm tempted to go all the way there, back inside "my" house. To "my room." To the comfy blanket and soft pillow left behind in the closet. It's too risky though.

The sun has set. The orange sky is now a soft purple. Soon it will be dark blue. The last reflection of sunlight glimmers off the clouds hugging the horizon. The first stars twinkle. I let gravity overtake me. Tears well up again. Silent. Salty-wet. It hurts. Everything hurts.

What if I close my eyes forever?

I don't usually think about stuff like that, but at this moment, in this time and space, I just... want to sleep. I want to not feel this pain.

Hope's cousin killed himself. Hope was a mess afterward. She didn't go to school for a few days. But when she returned, when she finally was able to talk about it, she said, "When you're alive, each day brings the promise of choice. Each day we choose to live. Even if it's hard. I wish my cousin had chosen to live."

I told her, "Maybe he couldn't see the choices."

"Maybe," she said.

It's hard to see what choices I have right now.

A shooting star blazes across the night sky. When my dad—my real dad—was alive, he was always so happy. I used to think about death a lot right after my dad's car accident. He didn't choose to die. He would have chosen to live, no matter what. Every morning, he'd say, "Thank the sun for shining and rising. Thank the Lord for another day of living!"

I was too young to know anything, but whenever I was sad, he'd remind me that it was only temporary.

All things are temporary.

Pain and sadness too.

Now, I think I understand what Hope was trying to say. I make my choice.

CHAPTER FOURTEEN

I wake to birds chirping. Despite the cold, I was able to sleep. I think crying as much as I did helped. Letting it all out. Every thought I was afraid to think, every emotion I was afraid to feel rushed out of me like a geyser.

I don't know if I'll be able to face Frank. I'm angry and scared still.

But I have made a choice. I'm going to give my presentation today. I don't really care about the consequences. I just want Mr. Christianson to hear what I've been working on. I know it's weird. I'm weird. But my paper is important to me. I spend the morning making it perfect.

I practice the whole way to school. When I walk into the classroom, everyone turns to look at me. Their stares make me feel more nervous.

Mr. Christianson looks startled when he sees me. His eyes are wide and confused at first and then worried. He moves around the room as if approaching a baby deer. It's clear to me he knows. I stare at him until his movements are steady. I know what I've done. He's going to turn me in now.

"I just want to give my report," I say, hoping he'll give me that at least.

"Presentation day," he says and nods at me. "Are you ready?"

"Yes," I say.

Mr. Christianson addresses the class. "Now remember, you all should have prepared notes for your talk. Hopefully a visual too, but it's not required. And a paper about your presentation."

I raise my hand. "I don't have a visual."

"It's all right, Luna," he says.

"And it's handwritten," I squeeze in.

He smiles, comforting and forgiving. "No worries, Luna. Handwritten on napkins will work too. Okay, scientists. Who's first?"

Only a single hand raises. It's the girl who knew the answer to Mr. Christianson's trick question on the first day of school. She has thick glasses. Her black hair is in braids. Her presentation is about how stars are formed. It's impressive. I don't really know her—I just know that she's smart. I've seen her with the other school nerds. The real nerds. The ones who are in school every day. They do all their homework and ace their exams. Overachievers. Not like me. I only wish I could spend more time on the school stuff.

I wait until everyone is finished. Butterflies flutter in my insides.

"Luna," Mr. Christianson says. "Are you ready?"

I nod. I'm the last one up. My classmates shift in their seats. Some whisper about me.

My presentation is on the formation of the moon. The giant-impact hypothesis. The moon formed during a large impact. When Earth was first forming, it collided with an object the size of Mars. What was left was a new but diminished Earth, the asteroid belt, and Earth's new companion, the moon.

I give my presentation with excitement, but I'm also nervous. I talk fast when I'm nervous.

The moment I open my mouth, it's like all the moisture is sucked out. My mouth is so dry, my throat pinches, but I manage to complete my presentation.

The class claps half-heartedly. Mr. Christianson applauds with gusto. He did that for all the presentations, but it still makes me feel good.

The bell rings. My classmates perk up. They chat while they exit the room. I'm about to leave when Mr. Christianson calls my name.

"Luna, do you have a sec?" he asks.

I nod.

He waits for the class to clear. When it's just him and me, he asks me a question I hoped to avoid. "What's going on? Everyone's been worried about you. Especially your mom."

"Not her," I say defiantly.

"Yes, her. I know it might be hard to understand your mom in your teenage years but..."

My eyes tear up. I don't think I can tell him.

"You don't have to tell me anything," he says. "But I think you should speak to someone. We have a counselor here."

"I don't want to get anyone in trouble," I say. As angry as I am, it's true. My mom, my sister, my brother... they love Frank. They need him. If I say something...

If I tell someone, I'll ruin everything.

"Did someone hurt you?" he asks.

I don't say anything. I stare at my feet, unsure of what to do.

"I know it seems like you're protecting the people you love, but if someone hurt you, it's not okay. And the people who love you want you to be safe and protected."

I want to say something, but I can't. I'm trapped by my silence.

Mr. Christianson continues, "Luna, the person who hurt you could hurt someone else too."

More tears come. My little sister. Sophie. I thought she might be safe because she's younger. Would Frank really do that to her too? The thought of it brings me a mixture of terror and guilt. "Can—can I speak to the counselor?"

"Yes," he says. "Let's go there now."

CHAPTER FIFTEEN

Talking with the counselor isn't as bad I thought it would be. A little awkward at first. She is kind and gentle. She explains to me about what Frank did. About it being a crime. It's not that I didn't know that already, but talking about it, especially with an adult, makes the reality of what happened sink in.

Then I wait for Mom. My foot is tapping like crazy. I can't stop it from moving even if I want to. The tapping helps me contain myself. As if I might burst open. We live about fifteen minutes from my school by car. I watch the clock tick at a snail's pace.

When she walks in, there's a heaviness in the room. I'm afraid to look at her. My mom and

I look alike. She's shorter and a shade or two darker, but we have the same eyes and nose. The same indent on the right side of our forehead.

"Luna?" Her voice cracks. Her eyes are red and puffy. She looks like a wreck. Worse than me. When our eyes meet, a sense of relief rolls over me. I feel like a little kid again. I launch out of my seat and she wraps her arms around me.

"Mom," I say, breaking down into a sob.

She cups my face in her hands. "What happened? Where were you?"

"Mrs. Davis," the counselor says. "Please, have a seat. Luna has something important to tell you."

Fear spreads across her face. "What is it, Luna? You're scaring me. Are you pregnant? I know there was that boy you liked. The one you and Hope were always gushing about."

"No, Mom," I say, annoyed. For a moment, I worry that what Frank did could have made me pregnant. It's too much to think about and I push it from my mind.

At first, I turn away, unable to look at her. But then, I make another choice. I lift my head and look my mom in the eyes.

I tell her what Frank did. Everything he did. I finally find the words and say them out loud:

He raped me.

Mom doesn't say anything at first.

"I'm... I don't know what to say," my mom says, hesitantly. Her voice is shaky. She doesn't even look at me. I wonder if that's *doubt* I hear in her words. Like she doubts I'm telling the truth.

"Mrs. Davis," the counselor interrupts. She puts her hand on my shoulder. "I have to report this. Luna cannot be released to your care until..."

"I know," my mom says, hanging her head. She finally looks at me. Her voice is still shaky and light. I almost can't hear her. "Luna, I love you." She looks right at me now. "And I believe you. I am so sorry."

"What's going to happen now?" I ask the counselor.

"A social worker is on her way to pick you up. The police will be notified, investigate what happened, and Frank may be arrested and formally booked and charged. As long as he is out of the home, you'll be able to go home. Otherwise, you'll have to stay in foster care. Do you understand?"

I nod.

She continues, "I'll give you two some privacy."

When she leaves, the office is quiet. I sit there silently too, playing with the pen in my hand. I wonder if my mom is mad at me. Maybe she just didn't want to make a scene. Then I see her in a reflection. There's a mirror across from us, and in it, I see that my mom is crying.

"Mom," I say. I put my hand on her shoulder.

She places her hand over mine. "I'm so sorry, Luna. I knew Frank could be a jerk, but I never thought he would do something like this."

"Neither did I. I mean, I knew he was creepy too, but I also never thought he'd..."

My mom is sobbing now. I hug her and say, "I'm sorry I left."

My mom pulls me to her. She lets her eyes catch mine, and cups my face again. "Never be sorry. He is wrong. Not you. He is at fault. Not *you*."

There's sincerity in her voice now. At least I want there to be. "I know," I say.

"You did nothing wrong. I only wish you would've told me from day one. I'm sorry you felt you needed to hide this from me. It's okay to not be okay. To be scared. Angry. Hurt. The important thing is that you're here now. Safe. And you spoke up. Always speak up. Never be afraid of the truth."

She hugs me tightly. I hug her tightly too. A different kind of hunger and sleepiness sets in. I just want to eat pizza. Curl up in my mom's arms. And cry.

"You'll be home soon because Frank is done. You don't ever have to worry about him."

"The twins?"

"The twins will be okay. They don't need a father like that. No one does. They love you. They love their sister. Just like I do." There's determination in her eyes. She's going to make this right.

"Mom?" I say.

"Yes?"

"I love you too."

EPILOGUE

Frank is out of the house. My mom only tells me what I need to know, but I overheard her say that he's out on bail. I think it scares my mom more than me. She's taking extra precautions. She makes sure a trusted adult is with the twins and me at all times. And she got a restraining order against Frank too.

Tonight is game night. Mom is home from work. We're playing Monopoly and watching old movies. Hope is reciting every word of *Pretty in Pink*. She can be an undercover nerd, though she'd never admit that. I'm more of a *Goonies* fan, but we both love cheesy '80s flicks.

"I never understood this part," I say. It's the part in the movie where Blane tells Andie he always believed in her, he just didn't believe in himself.

"I know, right," says Hope. "He keeps dodging her right before the dance. Funny way to believe in someone."

"Well, she *assumes* he's dodging her because she's poor," Sophie says. Hope and I are surprised Sophie butted in.

"You like this movie?" Hope asks.

"Not really, but I've been here every time you two have watched it." Sophie grabs a handful of popcorn and shoves it into her mouth.

We laugh, and I feel happy and sad at the same time. I wonder if I will always feel this way.

The doorbell rings. Mom ordered pizza. Two large pepperoni pies even though she hates pepperoni. Everyone surrounds the pizza like birds on a feeding frenzy. I bite into my slice so fast the cheese burns the roof of my mouth.

"How's therapy?" Hope asks as we walk back to the living room to pick up our *Monopoly* game where we left off.

It's a bit intrusive, but she claims Best Friend Rights, so I answer in my own way. I shrug. "Good."

I'm in therapy twice a week. My therapist and I talk about what happened. I like the journaling I've learned. A lot. I write in my journal every night about the events of the day, no matter how boring or exciting. I run too. Sometimes I laugh when I think about it because I did a lot of running when I left home. Now the running is good.

"Ha!" Mike says, standing over the *Monopoly* board, triumphant. "Pay up. Boardwalk with hotels."

He has a huge smile on his face. He has his hand out in front of Hope.

"No!" Hope groans. She pays him slowly, holding tightly to the money. He laughs. I wasn't sure Mike and Sophie would be okay with Frank leaving, but at least now I know they're safe.

I make a choice to let go. I won't ignore my sadness, but I can allow space to feel the happiness of the moment too.

Tonight the moon is full. I can see it from where I sit. I see its craters. Its flaws. Its history. A broken piece of rock that was once part of a beautiful planet. Its light is only a reflection of the sun. I used to wonder if the moon is following the Earth or running from it.

After our presentations, Mr. Christianson

spent a whole week on the moon. He taught us how much the moon helps the Earth. How it keeps the Earth's rotation from going all wonky. Now I know more. I know better.

I know now, the moon follows *me*. I marvel at her resilience. Her will to survive. To shine. Because after all, you need the moon to have moonlight. Most of all, the moon is not defined by her past.

She is the light in the dark.

WANT TO KEEP READING?

If you liked this book, check out another book
from West 44 Books:

BITTER & SWEET
BY DEMITRIA LUNETTA

ISBN: 9781538385234

AFTER

The cop is a woman. She doesn't look motherly or understanding. She looks mean. Mean and disgusted. Her suit is worn but clean.

They thought I would respond better to a woman. The truth is, I'll spill my guts to anyone who will listen. I feel the need to talk. It's like an itch I gotta scratch.

"We have to wait for your father to get here. You're a minor."

I shake my head. "My dad ain't gonna change nothin'. I killed the boy I loved most in the world."

She studies me, then leaves the interrogation room. I wonder how many people are watching me from the other side of that one-way mirror. Judging me. The way I talk. My torn jean shorts. The fading bruises on my arms. I sip my cola—the cheap stuff.

The cop returns with another, older woman. She has kind eyes and sensible brown shoes.

"Your father. He won't come. This is your appointed proxy guardian. Do you understand?"

I nod. Not surprised my daddy don't want nothing to do with me.

"You have to *say* you understand. For the tape." She pushes the table microphone toward me.

"I understand," I say. "This woman is here to make sure I don't say nothing stupid. But I don't need her. I'll tell you what happened if you want. I'll tell you all of it."

The women sit and wait for me to begin. Finally, I start.

"You have to understand," I say, my voice sounding desperate. I stop and take a deep breath. My shaking hand brings the soda can to my lips. I drink deeply, the sweet syrup taste helping to calm me.

I continue.

"Being in love with Tommy was like standing in line for a roller coaster. You're buzzing with excitement, but you're kind of fearful of what's coming. You also spend a lot of time hanging around for the payoff. And holy heck if it ain't worth the wait."

CHAPTER**ONE**

Three months ago

My stomach fills with eager dread as I push open the screen door to the rear of his house. Tommy's bedroom is back here. Even though it's three in the afternoon, he's probably just getting up. His school suspension hasn't fazed him at all.

Tommy says school ain't worth the time. There are plenty of ignorant people walking around with a high school diploma. School has always been hard for me, so I kinda agree with him on that.

"Tommy?" I call into the darkened house. I walk into the kitchen. My wet sneakers squeak on the floor. Then I go through to the living room. It rained during school and everything outside is covered in a thick slimy gloss. It shimmers in the afternoon heat.

I pause at his door. I hope he's not asleep. He won't like it if I wake him up. He'll be real mad. I take a step back. I'm about to retreat when I see him. A boy about Tommy's height but with dark brown hair instead of blond. "You ain't Tommy," I say stupidly.

"No... I'm not." He reaches over and switches on the living room light. It doesn't do much to brighten the house. Everything is old and worn and falling apart. Tommy doesn't come from money. Not that I do or anything.

For the first time I notice that the boy holds a knife in his hand. My stomach dips with fear.

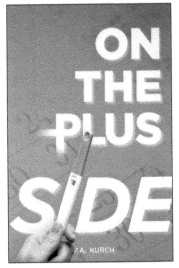

CHECK OUT MORE BOOKS AT:
www.west44books.com

An imprint of Enslow Publishing

WEST **44** BOOKS™

ABOUT THE AUTHOR

Cyn Bermudez is a writer, poet, and
artist living in Bakersfield, California.
She is the author of the hi-lo fiction
series, Brothers. She has a variety
of fiction and poetry publications in
magazines, journals, and anthologies
such as *Building Red: Mission Mars,
Perihelion SF, Strangelet, Middle
Planet,* and more. Please visit her
website for more information:
cynbermudez.com.